STADOLNIK

WILDLIFE ADVENTURE SERIES

RUFF

Illustrations by JOSEPH CAPOZIO

the wolf

WILLIAM S. BRISCOE

ADDISON-WESLEY PUBLISHING COMPANY

Menlo Park, California   Reading, Massachusetts   London   Don Mills, Ontario

TABLE OF CONTENTS

ONE EVENING long ago when I was a beginning teacher in Long Valley, I sat by the fire in a rundown hotel in Cascade. Suddenly I heard a long dismal howl. A chorus of howls followed. I had never heard wolves howl before, but the first thing I thought was that it must be a pack of wolves. I looked through the window at the swirling snow, fully expecting to see fifty wolves waiting outside the hotel—with me as their intended victim when I came out to walk home.

At that moment the desk clerk coughed, and I looked up to see him grinning at me.

"You don't seem very alarmed," I said.

In answer he turned to a tall man who had just entered the door and said, "Larry, the professor here is a bit nervous about the wolves in that willow thicket by the railroad track. He has to pass that way on his way back to the Diggs' house. He rooms there."

The tall man moved a chair over by the fire and began to tell me about wolves. The way he talked and what he said calmed my fears. Soon I found myself fascinated by the story of a most unusual gray timber wolf.

this is the story of that wolf

RUFF the wolf

1
THE WOLF DEN

JIM LOGUE paused at the top of the ridge and looked back down the trail. The sun was beginning to warm the western part of the small valley below. Somewhere near the two-story ranch house, a meadowlark was singing. Beyond the house and large red barn, fat healthy sheep grazed in the pasture. Winding its way through the valley was the Cascade River. It divided the Logue ranch into east and west ranges.

The small valley that held the sixteen-year-old boy's interest belonged to the Logues. It was really the northern tip of a longer valley that was called Long Valley. Long Valley stretched more than fifty miles to the south. From where Jim stood, however, the small valley seemed completely shut in by rolling grass-covered hills. Beyond the low hills were towering snow-capped mountains.

Jim studied the grazing sheep. In a short time, after the spring lambs were born, Jim would move the sheep from the valley and let them graze in the mountains. As he studied the wooly animals, Jim noted with satisfaction the number of black-faced sheep. He and his mother had spent a lot of money to buy six Hampshire rams in order to improve their flock. For the first time since his father's death, Jim felt that his father's dream of having a first-class sheep ranch was going to come true.

Just then something cold pressed against the boy's hand. Jim looked down at the large black-and-white collie at his feet. Queenie was the best sheep dog in Long Valley. When the dog saw that she held Jim's attention, she wagged her tail.

Jim knelt down and petted the border collie, but he looked back at the valley. All at once his eyes narrowed. A horse and rider were coming along the road that led to the ranch.

Jim jumped to his feet and gave a loud yell. The rider reined in his horse and looked up at the ridge. When he saw Jim, the horseman waved his hand. Then the man headed his horse up the trail to the ridge. A few minutes later Jim and the man were shaking hands.

"How are you, Mr. Harwood?" Jim said.

"Fine, Jim. I rode up here today to tell you that I might have a job for you."

"What is it?" the boy asked.

"Well," said Mr. Harwood, "I have reason to believe that there is a wolf den around here somewhere. I have never had time to look for it."

Jim nodded his head. "Some wolves do live in this part of the country. I've often seen a large white wolf and his mate in the mountains."

"I'd like you to try to find the den," Larry Harwood said. "I want to study the family life of wolves more closely. As you know, Jim, I am a professional naturalist for the United States government. The government wants to know more about wolves."

Jim smiled at Mr. Harwood. To the boy, Larry Harwood didn't look much like a naturalist—or as Jim thought a naturalist should look. The man was over six feet tall. With his broad shoulders and rugged features, he looked like a prize fighter.

"Do you think I can find the den?" the boy asked.

"I'm sure you can. Your high school principal says you can do almost anything you set your mind to."

"I'd like to, all right. If my mother approves, I'll start looking for the wolf den tomorrow."

Jim's mother did approve. So the next morning Jim set out with his pack containing a bedroll and food.

He carried his rifle under his arm with the muzzle pointing downward. At his side trotted Queenie. Jim traveled west at a steady pace through the woods and meadows. Not a breeze was stirring. The only sounds were the songs of meadowlarks and the chirping of insects. Between giant stands of pine and white fir were fields of tall grass. Here and there brightly colored wildflowers were starting to bloom.

Finally he came to a small stream. As the boy knelt down to drink, he saw some fresh tracks in the soft mud at the water's edge. They were longer and narrower than a dog's footprint. They were almost twice as large as a coyote's. Jim was sure that he had found some wolf tracks.

He looked around and studied the ground near the stream. A faint path of flattened grass led up the mountain. The trail had been made by the wild game that had wandered down from the high mountains to find water. Jim decided that this trail was also used by wolves. Mr. Harwood had told him that a wolf usually travels over the same route on his nightly hunts for food. This hunting trail is called a wolf runway.

Suddenly the border collie started whining and scratching at a clump of brush at the side of the path. From the way Queenie acted, Jim was sure that she had caught the scent of a wolf. The boy pulled a notebook out of his pocket and drew a rough map. Then he marked the trail on the map. On another page he wrote a brief description of the surrounding land.

Queenie found some more wolf scents that day. Jim began to feel that he knew quite a bit about the wolf runway. Still the boy had no idea where the wolves might have their den. He had filled his notebook with descriptions of the country near the runway. "But," he thought to himself, "what good are all these notes?"

Then he got an idea. "Where," he thought, "would a wolf be most likely to have a den?" Jim decided to pick out a few likely spots and watch them closely. This he did, but without success.

The following day Jim and Queenie followed the runway through a canyon and over a ridge to a long, narrow draw. Just as Jim and Queenie started through the draw, a small animal jumped out from under a shrub. It was a woodchuck. People in this part of the country called it a rockchuck.

Queenie crashed through the brush after the rockchuck. But the small furry animal raced up to a rocky ledge. There it sat up and scolded angrily. A few minutes later it had disappeared among the rocks.

Queenie, however, was no longer interested in chasing the rockchuck. Instead she was digging at a place among the rocks at the bottom of a cliff. Jim broke into a fast trot. When he reached the dog, he dropped to his knees. The lad let out a soft whistle as he saw what Queenie had uncovered. The dog had found a partly eaten carcass of a deer.

Jim was sure that the deer had been hidden there by the wolves. Jim noted the discovery in his book. Then the boy called to Queenie and started home. Tomorrow he would go to Cascade. He wanted to see what Larry Harwood would say about the discovery.

Early the next morning Jim saddled his horse and rode to Cascade. He found the naturalist at the hotel. For a long time Larry Harwood studied the notes. Finally he looked up, a pleased smile on his tan face. "Jim," he said, "this is a fine piece of work. In fact, for an amateur it is excellent!"

"But I haven't found the wolf den!" Jim answered.

"No, but you have found a plan. In science we call that research. Just keep on the way you have been doing. It may take longer than you imagined, but I am sure you will succeed.

"By the way," he said, glancing down at the book, "I think you have found a wolf cache."

"What's that?" the boy asked.

"That deer carcass was hidden by the wolf for a later meal. Possibly it was put there by the male wolf for his mate. If the female has whelps, or pups, at the den, she won't leave the den to go hunting. The male wolf has to keep her supplied with food."

"Does that mean that the wolf den might be near the cache?" Jim asked hopefully.

"The wolf den could be within a mile of the cache," Mr. Harwood replied.

"A mile covers a lot of territory, but I guess it's better than thirty miles!" the boy replied. He was thinking of the length of the runway he had followed so far.

Larry Harwood grinned. "A wolf runway may be over a hundred miles long!"

"Wow! I guess I'm lucky that Queenie found that cache!"

Mr. Harwood was amused. "Wolves choose dens that *can't* be easily seen. Their dens are so well concealed that you could walk right by one and not even notice it."

Seeing that the boy was discouraged, Larry Harwood added kindly, "I just wanted you to see the wolves' point of view. Here's a hint to help you in your search. Wolves like to see what's going on around them. Possibly the den might be on a high ledge or near the top of a cliff. I see in your notes that you have described a rock slide in a ravine. You might watch it."

Jim decided to follow Mr. Harwood's advice and watch the rock slide. So the next day Jim went back to the draw where he had found the cache. He told Queenie to stay at the bottom of the draw. Then he slowly climbed the steep slope. At the top he found a high rock that made a kind of lookout point. Trying not to make any noise, he crawled forward to the edge of the high rock. Beneath him was a narrow ravine filled with large boulders. The opposite side of the ravine rose gradually to a long narrow ledge.

Although Jim didn't see him, an old white male wolf was lying on the shadowy ledge. The wolf fixed his slanting yellow eyes on the boy's face. To call attention to himself and away from his den, the large white animal slowly rose to his feet. Then he circled a few times. Finally he curled up in a ball as if to sleep. All the time he watched Jim closely.

Jim, however, did not notice the white wolf. His eyes were fixed on a spot in the rock slide. The boy was so surprised, he almost gasped out loud. From the high rock on which he lay, he saw a steel-gray wolf. The gray wolf was dozing between two large boulders that led to a den in the rocks. Nearby, five pups crawled around. The gray wolf was a female with whelps!

To Jim, the whelps looked more like rats than baby wolves. They were all the same color—sort of a dirty brown. They had fuzzy coats and thin wispy tails.

Then one of the pups, bigger than all the rest, fought his way to his mother's side. Shoving and pushing the other pups, the big pup managed to get the best place for lunch for himself. After the whelps had finished nursing, the female drowsily licked their stomachs. She pressed their stomachs with her nose. Filled by the rich, warm milk, the little whelps had already fallen into a deep sleep. Finally, the female stretched out lazily in the sun and went back to sleep.

Because Jim had not moved, neither had the white wolf. Still, the wolf had kept his eyes fast upon Jim. Neither he nor the boy noticed a man with a rifle slipping through the brush along the ledge.

A minute later a loud blast echoed through the ravine. The whelps, whimpering in terror, started crawling blindly about. As Jim watched in horror, one after another of the little pups was shot. The female could not help her young. The first bullet had pierced her heart.

The male dashed up to a high rock above the ledge. There he started howling, trying to distract the gunman's attention. Then a bullet hit the male wolf's leg. The animal let out a startled yelp and disappeared from sight. All was silence.

Jim, his head still reeling from shock, slowly got to his feet. At his side was Queenie. She had raced up the slope at the first gun shot. Then Jim saw a tall, weatherbeaten man leaning against a rock. The man's gun was still smoking.

Mr. Diggs looked over at Jim. Then he pushed back his hat and pulled out the bolt of his rifle and blew down the barrel.

"Howdy, Jim," the rancher said in a friendly voice. "Too bad the white one got away."

"You had no right to kill these wolves," Jim said, his voice shaking in anger. "Only *our* stock graze in this section of the mountains."

If Mr. Diggs was surprised at Jim's words, he did not show it. Instead, the rancher climbed down the slope to the den. Then he calmly started to skin the gray female wolf.

After a while the rancher said, "The mountains are still open range, boy." Seeing that Jim was not going to say anything, the rancher went on. "Seems to me that you would be glad to see these wolves dead. Wolves are becoming a problem around here."

"Wolves weren't a problem when my father was alive," the boy replied curtly.

Mr. Diggs looked over and studied the boy. The gray-haired rancher liked what he saw—a frank, honest face; intelligent blue eyes; strong, broad shoulders; a body toughened by years of hard work. Like his father, the Logue boy had plenty of courage and spirit.

"When your father was alive," Mr. Diggs said finally, "things were different. Now more and more people are settling down in this part of the country. They are raising more cattle and sheep. That means, of course, less wild game. When the big game animals disappear, the wolves and other predators will have no choice except to kill livestock for food."

Mr. Diggs carried the pelt of the gray female up to the ledge and back to where his horse was standing. Like most western horses, his horse had been trained to stand where it was when the reins were dropped. The horse snorted when Mr. Diggs slung the pelt over its back, but it did not move.

As he tied the pelt firmly to the saddle, the rancher continued talking. "Son, it's my job to know wolves. I have plenty of respect for them, too. The question is, who is going to live in this country—the wolves or the ranchers? It's not big enough for both!"

Jim knew that in a way Frank Diggs was right. Still, the boy regretted that, in a country as large as this, some room couldn't have been found for the old gray female and her young.

The tall rancher mounted his horse and looked at Jim. "Mark my words, boy," he said. "The wolf problem is going to get worse. When the wolves start eating your sheep, you'll hunt them down fast enough!" Then he trotted his horse out of the ravine.

For a few minutes Jim stood staring thoughtfully after the rancher. Then the boy realized that Queenie was acting strangely. The border collie was whining and scratching near the boulders on the other side of the ravine.

Jim made his way quickly to Queenie's side and laid his hand on her head. "What's wrong, girl?" he asked.

At Jim's words, Queenie crawled into an opening between the rocks and disappeared. A moment later she reappeared. But the black-and-white dog was not alone. Held firmly in her mouth was a brown furry wolf pup!

Jim took the whimpering pup from Queenie and slid it inside his jacket. This seemed to comfort the whelp because it stopped crying.

At that moment a long, wailing howl rang out. All this time the white male had waited uneasily out of sight. Now the old wolf was calling to his mate and whelps. In answer, the pup under Jim's jacket whimpered. Then Jim turned and started on the long walk back to the ranch. As he did so, another mournful howl echoed through the narrow ravine.

2
A NEW HOME

WHEN JIM walked into the house, Mrs. Logue was setting the table. Smiling fondly at her son, the tall slender woman said, "Better wash up. Supper is almost ready."

For a second Jim hesitated at the door. Mrs. Logue, feeling that something was wrong, looked closely at her son. "What is it?" she asked, puzzled.

"Oh, nothing," Jim said nonchalantly, "except that I found an animal." The boy patted the side of his jacket.

Mrs. Logue eyed Jim suspiciously. Across her mind flashed the steady stream of wildlife that Jim had been bringing home ever since he could walk. Mrs. Logue, remembering her son's pet spiders and snakes, shuddered slightly and glanced apprehensively at the bulge under Jim's jacket.

"Well," she said, putting her hands on her hips, "what is it?"

"Just a little male wolf pup," Jim replied, trying to sound unconcerned.

"You mean to say," Sadie Logue said, her clear blue eyes suddenly growing dark, "you brought a vicious wolf into this house?"

Jim didn't say anything. Instead he reached inside his jacket and pulled out the sleeping pup. Disturbed by the sudden movement, the pup started to whimper.

For a moment Mrs. Logue just stared at the furry brown ball. The pup didn't seem any larger than her son's hand. Then she suddenly smiled.

"I must say he certainly doesn't look very vicious, does he?" she said at last. Her face softened as she gazed at the little pup.

Knowing that his mother had accepted this new pet, Jim walked over and put the pup in his mother's hands.

"My goodness," Mrs. Logue said, looking at the pup's tiny wrinkled face. "His eyes aren't even open! Do you know what that means?"

Jim nodded. "It means that the whelp is probably not more than a week old."

"It also means that you will have to feed him milk out of a bottle every several hours. And that means feeding him in the middle of the night," said Mrs. Logue.

Jim nodded his head. He had gone through the early morning feeding last year when he had brought home a young fawn whose mother had been shot.

Jim got out some nipples and a bottle. Then he started heating up some milk. Mrs. Logue was trying to comfort the whelp, which was whimpering loudly.

When the milk was warm, Jim poured it into the bottle and picked up the little pup. After a few feeble licks, the little pup's toothless gums clamped down on the nipple, and he started sucking the warm milk.

While Jim fed the pup, Mrs. Logue got out a small box and filled it with some wool and soft cloth.

"There," she said, standing back and looking at her work. "That box will be the whelp's den."

When the little pup had finished the milk, Jim put the pup into the box. The whelp snuggled into the wool and went to sleep. He was so full of milk that his stomach looked as though it might burst.

"What are you going to call the pup?" Mrs. Logue asked Jim as they sat down to supper.

"I've thought of a name," Jim said. "How about 'Ruff'?"

"That's a nice name," Sadie Logue answered, "but why 'Ruff'?"

"Well," Jim replied, "Mr. Harwood told me that male wolves have a thick collar of hair, or a ruff, around their necks."

At that moment a loud shrill cry rang out. Jim dropped his fork and ran over to the box. Ruff was crawling around, groaning in pain.

"I wonder what's the matter with him?" Jim asked as the puppy's cries seemed to get louder.

"Maybe he got some air in his stomach when he was sucking the bottle," Jim's mother suggested. "Maybe you should burp him!"

Jim tried burping Ruff over his shoulder like a baby. But that did not work. Still the pup cried. Then Jim had an idea. He went to the door and called Queenie.

When Queenie came into the house, she sniffed the whimpering pup. She seemed to know what was wrong because she pushed the pup down and started to lick his stomach. She pressed his stomach with her nose. In a few minutes Ruff burped. Then he curled up beside Queenie and went to sleep.

Mrs. Logue and Jim looked at each other and smiled.

"Well, Ruff looks more like a dog than a wolf!" Mrs. Logue said. "I believe Queenie thinks the whelp *is* a dog!"

In a few days Ruff's eyes had opened. They were a dusky blue. Although the pup would not be able to see well for another week, Ruff was wobbling around the kitchen floor. He followed Queenie, trying to catch her long tail. Sometimes he bumped into walls and chairs and tumbled over.

By September, Ruff was four months old. He had changed considerably. His dark fuzzy hair had turned to a sleek gray coat. His muzzle was slimmer, and his eyes had turned from blue to yellow. He was almost three feet long from his nose to the tip of his tail. His long legs, big feet, and large head seemed much too big for his body. In spite of his awkward appearance, the wolf was very graceful.

Next to the barn Jim had built a large runway of chicken wire so that Ruff could stay outside without being chained. When Jim and Queenie were tending the sheep, Ruff was kept in the pen. He liked to be in the pen better than he liked to be chained. If Jim chained him to the porch, Ruff would lift his head to the sky and howl forlornly. Jim would not let Ruff run loose for fear that coyotes might kill him.

Every afternoon Jim took Ruff and Queenie for a walk. It was always a slow walk because the curious pup had to sniff at every tree, rock, and bush. He wanted to make sure that no strange animal had been there since his last visit.

On the afternoon walks, Jim usually stopped at a grassy clearing in the woods where a fat old rockchuck lived.

Ever since Queenie had taught Ruff how to sniff for rockchucks, the wolf had been trying to catch this particular chuck. But the old rockchuck was very wise. As a matter of fact, the old fellow seemed to enjoy having Ruff chase him.

Jim laid his hand on Queenie's head and sat down on a fallen log to watch the fun. The boy did not have long to wait. Ruff was carefully sniffing the ground. All at once the old rockchuck darted through the grass, the barking wolf on his trail. When the little animal was a safe distance away, the rockchuck sat up and started scolding in sharp little whistles. It seemed to Jim that the little fellow was calling Ruff names in rockchuck language. Then the fat old animal disappeared into his den.

The hair around the wolf's neck stood straight up. Jim knew that this was a sign that Ruff was very angry. Angry as he was, however, the wolf finally had to give up. But no sooner had the wolf started back towards Jim than the rockchuck stuck his head out of his burrow and called the wolf more names.

Suddenly Queenie dashed off. When the dog came near the place where the rockchuck usually fed, she dropped to the ground. She lay so flat that she could hardly be seen.

Ruff cocked his head and watched. Then he bounded after Queenie and dropped to the ground beside her.

After a while the rockchuck stuck his nose out of his den. He didn't see any danger, so the old fellow came out of his den and sat up. He gave a sharp whistle. Queenie did not move. Neither did Ruff.

Finally the fat old rockchuck went to his feeding ground and began to eat. When he was a good distance from his den, Queenie sprang after him.

The rockchuck raced away, but Queenie was too fast. After she caught him, Queenie let Ruff have the rock-chuck. Ruff growled and shook him. He shook the rockchuck as hard as he could, growling all the time. Ruff seemed to be getting even for the rockchuck names he had been called.

Strangely enough, after he had given the rockchuck a good shaking, the wolf let him go. Without stopping once, the rockchuck dashed across the meadow and into the woods.

When Jim got home that evening, he told his mother about the hunting lesson that Queenie had given Ruff. "But," the boy added after he had told the story, "I just can't understand why Ruff let that rockchuck go!"

"Why should he want to eat a tough, old rockchuck?" Mrs. Logue said sarcastically. "After all, he can have all the tender, juicy lamb roast, steak, and stew that he wants. Not only that, if he keeps eating the way he has been, I'm going to have to spend the whole day just cooking for him!"

Jim chuckled and said, "Remember, Mom, Ruff is just a growing pup."

"*I* know he's just a growing pup, but does *he* know it? Already he eats more food than a dozen horses. In fact I think he could eat the dozen horses, too, and *still* be hungry."

Ruff caught many more rockchucks during the next several weeks. To him, hunting rockchucks was a game. But after a while Ruff grew tired of catching rockchucks. It was too easy!

One afternoon Jim rode into Cascade to visit Mr. Harwood. He left Ruff and Queenie at home. As the day wore on, Ruff began to get nervous. He knew it was time for his walk. Restlessly the wolf paced back and forth in his pen. Finally he sat down and started to howl.

Mrs. Logue came out of the house to see what was the matter with Ruff. Glancing at the sun, she said aloud, "I know it's time for your walk, but Jim isn't back yet."

Ruff whined and jumped up against the side of the pen, and Mrs. Logue opened the gate. "It's such a nice day," she said. "I'm going to let you run with Queenie a while."

Ruff raced out of his pen, and he and Queenie chased each other around the yard. First Queenie would chase Ruff, and then he would chase her. They rolled over and over, growling and barking at each other. This was a sport they both loved.

Suddenly Ruff turned and started running up the trail.

"Ruff!" Mrs. Logue cried. "Come back, Ruff. Come back!"

But Ruff just kept running farther up the trail. Queenie had stayed in the yard, but now she, too, started up the trail. The collie ran as fast as she could to catch up with the wolf. Finally both wolf and dog disappeared from sight.

For a long time Mrs. Logue stood staring up the empty trail. Finally she said in a soft whisper, "Take care of him, Queenie. Take care of him for Jim."

Then the woman turned and went back into the house to wait for Jim to come home.

3
TRAPPED!

WHEN RUFF AND QUEENIE got tired of playing, they hunted for rabbits. As the afternoon passed, the dog and wolf, traveling in a wide half circle through the mountains, had come to the Cascade River. They were about ten miles downstream from the Logue ranch.

As Queenie and Ruff made their way through the brush, they saw a cottontail. They chased it into a small willow thicket at the river's edge. The thicket was so dense that neither Ruff nor Queenie could get through it. But Queenie had taught Ruff how to catch rabbits as well as rockchucks. By working together as a team, the wolf and dog had caught many rabbits.

Queenie crouched near the spot where the cottontail had disappeared. Ruff turned and ran down the path next to the thicket, searching for an opening. Finally Ruff found a narrow entrance to the thicket. He sniffed the ground around the opening. The scents told him many things. He knew rabbits and coyotes had been there. He could also smell fresh blood.

The smell of blood excited him, and Ruff started into the narrow tunnel-like opening. But he didn't get far! Suddenly something snapped around his left leg. The wolf was jerked to the ground. A terrible pain ran through his leg. Ruff jumped up, but again he was thrown to the ground. The wolf let out a shrill yelp, almost like a scream. Then he started to bite and snap at the strange-looking thing that held his right hind leg.

At Ruff's cry, Queenie knew that something was wrong. With a bark she ran down the path to the opening. She saw at once that Ruff was caught in a trap. The wolf was no longer struggling. He had learned that to fight the thing on his leg meant pain. If he lay still, he felt only a dull ache. When the wolf saw Queenie, he whined a mournful greeting.

Queenie was wise in the trapping methods of the ranchers. She smelled dead coyote and dead rabbit. Using rabbits for bait, someone had been trapping coyotes. Queenie knew there might be other traps about. She looked very carefully at everything. Not a blade of grass missed her sharp eyes.

Queenie moved forward cautiously and dropped down at Ruff's side. She licked his face and the leg that was held fast by the trap. Her presence seemed to comfort the wolf, for he stopped whimpering.

Suddenly a coyote came warily down the path along the thicket. When Queenie saw it, she crouched at Ruff's side and watched.

The coyote stared at the dog and wolf. No dog had ever acted like this before. The animal was so curious that it started moving toward Queenie and Ruff.

With a deep growl Queenie sprang toward the coyote. Her teeth sunk into its flank. Jumping on top of it, she closed her jaws on the coyote's throat. Queenie could have easily killed the animal, but she let it go. Yelping like any injured dog, the coyote fled. Queenie knew it would not come back.

Then Queenie turned and ran up the riverbank to the dirt road that ran along it. There she started to bark— first slow, loud, and deep—then high, fast, and sharp. She had learned this while working with sheep. To Jim and the other ranchers, this was a sort of language they understood. It meant that something was wrong!

After barking for a while, Queenie went back to see if Ruff was all right. The wolf whined softly when he saw her, but he did not struggle to get up. Queenie sat down beside him and licked his face. After a while she turned and went back to the trail.

Suddenly a wagon appeared in the distance. For a moment the driver stopped the wagon and sat listening. Then he sent the horses into a fast gallop. A few yards from the collie, the driver stopped the team.

Mr. Diggs looked down at Queenie. "What is it, old girl?" he asked. "Is someone hurt?"

Queenie barked happily and wagged her tail when she saw Mr. Diggs. Turning, she ran down the bank. Then she stopped and barked at the rancher.

As Mr. Diggs got down from the wagon, it suddenly occurred to him that Jim Logue might be in some kind of trouble. He grabbed his rifle and quickly followed the barking dog. He walked carefully, avoiding the traps he had set up near the thicket a few days ago. As he came to the opening in the thicket, he stopped in amazement when he saw the wolf.

Ruff curled up his lips and growled at the rancher. But Queenie whined and wagged her tail. She licked Ruff's face. The dog trusted the rancher. She tried to make Ruff understand that the rancher was there to help. Although Ruff did not like this man's scent, he finally stopped growling and lay quietly.

Mr. Diggs lifted his rifle to his shoulder and aimed it carefully at the wolf's head. Queenie was sitting next to Ruff, her ears pricked forward in curiosity. Her trusting eyes never left the rancher's face.

Something about Queenie's manner made Mr. Diggs change his mind. Finally he lowered the gun. He couldn't understand why Jim's collie seemed so friendly with a wolf. The man's thoughts went back to his last meeting with the young Logue boy.

"By golly," the rancher said, snapping his fingers. "I think that young fellow probably found one of the old steel-gray wolf's pups that I missed. I've heard of tame wolves, but I've never seen one."

The rancher kept on talking in a low voice so that the wolf would get used to him. At the same time he moved a step closer. Ruff still did not move. Then suddenly the wolf started to wag his tail.

"You *act* friendly enough. I certainly hope you *are* friendly," Mr. Diggs said gently. He slowly stretched out his hand. Mr. Diggs knew that even though the wolf was young, the whelp had sharp teeth and powerful jaws. The rancher could easily lose a few of his fingers!

Seeing that the wolf was not going to harm him, the gray-haired man knelt down and sprang the trap. Then he examined the wolf's leg.

"You'll never make it home," he said, shaking his head. "If you'll let me carry you, I'll drive you home in my wagon."

Mr. Diggs hesitated for a second and then picked up the wolf. With Queenie trotting happily at his side, the rancher carried Ruff out of the thicket.

When Mr. Diggs drove into the ranch yard, Mrs. Logue had just finished telling Jim that Ruff had run away. Jim was so surprised to see Ruff sitting in the wagon that the boy could not speak.

Mr. Diggs pulled the team of horses to a stop and took off his hat. "How are you, Sadie?" he asked, ignoring Jim's questioning look.

"Fine, Frank. But where did you find Ruff?" she asked. Mrs. Logue was just as surprised as Jim.

"Oh, he got himself caught in one of my coyote traps near the river. I don't think his leg is too badly hurt."

As the rancher helped Jim get Ruff out of the wagon, Mrs. Logue asked, "Frank, won't you come in and have supper with us?"

"Your cooking is famous throughout the valley, Sadie. I wouldn't miss the chance."

"I see you haven't changed much, Frank Diggs!" Mrs. Logue said scoldingly, blushing at the man's compliment.

While Mrs. Logue prepared supper, Mr. Diggs watched as Jim cleaned and bound the wolf's wounded leg. When Jim was through, Ruff grabbed Jim's arm between his powerful jaws.

Mr. Diggs grunted, and Jim looked up.

"Don't worry, sir," Jim told the surprised rancher. "This is Ruff's way of showing his affection."

Mr. Diggs stirred and said, "I've heard of wolves that have been tamed. Wolves are supposed to be a lot smarter than dogs."

Jim nodded his head. "Ruff is smart, all right. You never have to show him how to do the same thing twice. Queenie's a pretty intelligent dog, but even she isn't *that* smart."

The rancher nodded his head thoughtfully. A few minutes later he said, "I hear that part-Hampshire ewe of yours had twins. Do we have time to take a look?"

"Sure!" Jim said, jumping to his feet. "Come on!"

"You were right in buying those Hampshires," Mr. Diggs said a few minutes later. Together he and Jim watched a handsome pair of lambs frisk around in the sheep pen. "At first I thought you and your mother were crazy to spend so much money on six sheep. But I don't think so now. Before long you are going to have the best sheep in the whole valley."

Suddenly the rancher turned and looked Jim straight in the eyes. "That wolf of yours seems tame enough now. But what will you do if he decides to help himself to a meal now and then?" the rancher said solemnly, and pointed toward the sheep.

"Ruff has never even growled at a sheep, sir," Jim replied indignantly. "He *wouldn't* kill a sheep!"

"I hope you're right," the rancher said. Then he turned and started back toward the house.

For a few minutes Jim stood gazing at the lambs, Mr. Harwood's words ringing in his ears. Then the boy turned and ran to catch up with the gray-haired rancher.

4
MORE TROUBLE

FOR A LONG TIME Ruff's leg was sore, and the wolf limped. But by the time winter was over, Ruff was as good as ever. The wolf was no longer kept in a pen but was allowed to roam freely. He was well able to take care of himself. His powerful jaws and sharp teeth could easily snap the life out of most animals. He was a year old now. He stood twenty-seven inches high at the shoulder. He weighed over one hundred pounds.

Although the wolf was quite a bit larger and heavier than Queenie, he and the collie still played together. But now Queenie always lost their make-believe fights. Still, the collie did not mind. On the contrary, she seemed to be very proud of the big pup she had raised.

One bright spring morning, Larry Harwood rode up to the ranch. Jim and Mrs. Logue were glad to see him. Neither of them had been to Cascade since the beginning of winter. But Larry's usually happy face looked troubled.

"Do you know," he asked them, "that the Long Valley Stockmen's Association is going to start assessing each member ten cents for each head of livestock? The money is going to be used to pay hunters a bounty for each wolf and coyote they kill."

Jim flashed Ruff a worried look. He didn't want some hunter to take a shot at his wolf. Jim asked Mr. Harwood, "When did the association decide to do that?"

"At the meeting last week. I tried to talk the ranchers out of it," the rugged naturalist said. He glanced up at the high mountain peaks. "I told them that there would be trouble if they started destroying all the wolves and coyotes. I pointed out that the coyotes help the farmers by killing rabbits and other pests. I told them the wolves keep the wild game strong and healthy by killing the weak and diseased animals. But they wouldn't listen. Even though they lose more livestock from disease, floods, droughts, and other causes, the ranchers seemed to be incensed about the wolves and coyotes."

"We've never had trouble with wolves before," Sadie Logue said.

"The coyotes and a few wolves are coming down from the high mountains. So many game animals are being slaughtered by hunters that the coyotes and wolves are coming to the valley to find food. A lot of livestock was killed by predators this winter."

"It's strange that we didn't lose any stock," Jim said.

"Well, you have a good watchdog there." Mr. Harwood smiled and pointed to Ruff. "No coyote is going to tackle that wolf! Just remember, be careful when you take the wolf tramping through the woods with you. Keep your eyes open for dead animals that might have been poisoned. Also, watch out for traps and stray bullets!"

Jim, however, had nothing to worry about when it came to traps. Ruff had never forgotten his experience with the steel trap. With Queenie's help he quickly learned how to find and avoid other traps.

One afternoon on their regular walk, Jim stopped to tie his shoe. Queenie and Ruff raced on ahead. Suddenly Queenie stopped and sniffed the air. Something was wrong. Ruff had smelled it, too. Instead of stopping, however, the wolf bounded forward. There on a rocky ledge were two dead coyotes and a dead sheep.

Ruff had never paid any attention to the sheep on the Logue ranch, but somehow this sheep was different. The smell of blood was strong as Ruff sniffed the wooly animal. Besides, he was very hungry.

Queenie approached the ledge more cautiously than Ruff. To her, the scent was not right. She growled at Ruff, but he ignored her and went on smelling the sheep.

Queenie growled again and walked up to Ruff. Now the wolf began to get angry at Queenie. He bared his teeth and laid back his ears, but Queenie would not move. Then he crouched low and snarled savagely. At that moment Queenie charged!

Ruff could have easily killed Queenie, but something within him held him back. Maybe it was the tie of friendship that had grown strong between Queenie and Ruff. The wolf's teeth closed firmly but gently upon the dog's throat. Over and over the dog and wolf rolled until they were at the edge of the ledge. Then Queenie lost her balance and fell off the ledge. Ruff watched as the dog rolled down the steep slope. Then he went to the sheep and began to eat.

When Queenie got to her feet, she noticed Jim climbing up the slope. Barking and whining, she ran down to meet him.

"Queenie, are you trying to tell me something?" the boy asked.

44

Queenie barked and started running back up the slope. Jim quickly followed her. At the top of the ledge the boy found the dead sheep and the coyotes. Nearby lay Ruff.

Queenie approached Ruff and sniffed him. Ruff opened his eyes and lifted his head. Then his head fell back. The wolf had been poisoned! Someone had put poison tablets in the dead sheep to kill predators!

Jim was scared. He put his arms around Ruff and lifted the groaning wolf to his feet. Being on his feet made Ruff feel even sicker. He felt so sick that he vomited. He vomited again and again.

"That's good," Jim thought to himself. "It will help get rid of some of the poison."

Then Jim lifted Ruff up and started down the steep slope. It was hard work carrying the heavy wolf. By the time he reached the bottom, the boy was exhausted. Jim knew he could never get Ruff home.

"Queenie," he said, "you stay here and guard Ruff. I'll get the wagon. Stay, Queenie!"

Queenie watched Jim disappear around the bend. Then she walked over to Ruff and licked the wolf's face.

Just then three coyotes came out of the timber on the side of the hill. Queenie's fur bristled along her neck and she growled. The coyotes, hearing the dog's growl, stretched up their bodies. They started walking stiff-legged down the hill.

Suddenly the breeze shifted. The coyotes caught the scents of the dead sheep and coyotes on the high ledge. The smells seemed strange. They also smelled the dog and wolf. This was very strange indeed. They turned and ran back towards the timber. At the edge of the woods they stopped and looked back again. Then they disappeared into the timber.

Jim ran all the way back to the ranch house. Panting for breath, he gasped to his mother, "Ruff has been poisoned. Help me hitch up the team."

Mrs. Logue was wearing dungarees, which she would never wear anywhere except on the ranch. But she didn't take time to change her clothes.

As she and Jim ran to the barn, she said, "We'd better take the buckboard. It'll be faster."

Quickly they hitched up the horses. They climbed to the seat of the buckboard. Then Jim cracked the whip, and the horses galloped off at a dead run. Mrs. Logue hung onto the seat with both hands. Even so, she was bounced up and down on the seat as Jim recklessly drove up the trail.

"Jim," Mrs. Logue gasped. "For goodness' sake, slow down! You will wreck us and maybe break our necks!"

46

But the woman's warning came too late. Just then the right rear wheel hit a large boulder hidden in grass at the side of the road. There was the sound of splintering wood. Then the buckboard started to turn over.

Jim pulled back on the reins to stop the horses from running away. Mrs. Logue clung to the side of the buckboard to keep from falling out. The seat was slanted up at a dangerous tilt.

When the horses stood quietly, Mrs. Logue jumped out. She held the reins while Jim got out. Together they looked at the damage.

"The right rear wheel is shattered," Jim cried. "We'll never make it now. We'll never make it!"

"Take it easy, son," Sadie Logue said calmly as she looked at the buckboard. Then she added, "Well, that's that! But we should be able to bring Ruff home on a horse. You fetch that blanket on the seat."

Jim looked at his mother in amazement as she started unhitching the team. "We don't have any saddles," he reminded her.

"Oh, pshaw," Mrs. Logue said. "Give me a leg up."

The next instant she was astride the horse and galloping off. Jim had to ride fast to catch up with her.

When Jim and his mother came in sight, Queenie barked happily and ran to meet them. When they reached Ruff's side, the wolf looked more dead than alive. His tongue was hanging out, and he was panting.

As Mrs. Logue and Jim knelt by his side, Ruff opened his eyes and tried to get up.

"It's all right, fellow," Mrs. Logue said. She patted Ruff's head. Looking up at Jim, she said, "Spread that blanket out on the ground. Help me wrap it around Ruff."

Then Mrs. Logue and Jim carried Ruff over to the horses. Both of the horses were broken to western customs. As long as the reins were down, they would stand. Both animals had also carried deer and other game on their backs.

Together Jim and his mother managed to get Ruff onto one of the horses. Mrs. Logue balanced Ruff until Jim was mounted behind the wolf.

Then Mrs. Logue led her horse over to some boulders. Standing on one of them, she climbed on the horse. Then she grabbed the reins of Jim's horse and led the way down the slope.

Suddenly Jim noticed that his mother was not heading towards the ranch. "Where are you going, Mom?" he called.

"To the river. This wolf needs water—lots of it!"

When they came to the river, Jim carried Ruff into the shallow water. Ruff was desperate for water. He began to drink. The wolf drank for a long time. Finally he began to cough. Jim felt him trembling. Then Ruff started to vomit up the water.

Mrs. Logue nodded her head in approval. "Let him drink some more."

After a while, Jim and his mother carried Ruff back to the horses and headed home.

For the next week Ruff's life was in danger. Mrs. Logue hovered over him constantly. Every few hours she would force a mixture of milk and eggs into the wolf's mouth. Finally Ruff began to get stronger.

One evening as Mrs. Logue sat in her rocking chair, Ruff took his first wobbling steps. He walked slowly over to her and laid his head on her lap.

Mrs. Logue put her hand on Ruff's head. "I think Ruff is trying to thank me," she said.

Jim came over and put one arm around his mother and the other around Ruff.

"He is thanking you," Jim said. "And I do, too."

Sadie smiled at her son, and then she laid her cheek on Ruff's head.

Queenie, wanting to get some attention too, came over and pushed her head under Jim's arm. Jim laughed and hugged her. The Logue family was safely together again.

5

THE BLACK WOLF

THE FOLLOWING DAYS were happy ones for Ruff and Jim. The boy's love for his wolf companion deepened and was matched by Ruff's genuine fondness for the boy. Jim was never happier than when he was tramping through the woods and meadows with Ruff and Queenie romping by his side. During the summer Queenie and Jim taught Ruff how to tend the sheep. Even Mr. Harwood was surprised when he learned that Ruff could herd sheep.

Another year passed. Again the grass turned brown as summer passed over the valley. Then came the cooling breezes of autumn. Many of the trees turned red and yellow and even purple. There was a riot of color along the river's edge. Finally the full force of winter was upon the land. For weeks the snow fell. Soon the mountains and valleys were covered by a huge white quilt.

In some places the wind piled the snow into giant drifts. Where the wind had uncovered patches of grass, herds of deer and elk could be found grazing on the lower meadows and in Long Valley. The wild game had drifted down from the high mountains where food had become scarce.

The ranchers of the valley were worried. Never before had there been so few deer or elk. The ranchers knew that mountain lions, coyotes, and wolves would soon follow the big game to the lower ridges and to the valley. Soon the wailing cries of wolves could be heard in the night. Before long most of the ranchers were losing sheep and cattle and young horses.

The Logues, however, were not losing any livestock at all. Ruff saw to that. He was almost three years old. He was thirty-five inches high at the shoulder and was five feet long. He weighed one hundred fifty pounds. To the wolf, the Logue ranch was *his* ranch. Every evening he would check the boundaries. At a smooth trot he would pace the small valley. He made sure that no stranger had visited his land since the night before.

One bright moonlight night Ruff was again checking the boundaries. As he trotted along the northern section of the valley, he suddenly caught a strange scent. He followed the scent to a clump of trees. There stood a wolf. Her black coat blended with the dark trees so that she was almost invisible.

Ruff came forward at a stiff-legged walk, his lips curled back in a snarl. The black wolf did not seem afraid. As Ruff came closer and closer, she suddenly sank down on the ground and whined.

Ruff stopped, surprised. Since the day Jim had carried him away from the wolf den where he was born, Ruff had never met a wolf. He did not know what to do. Finally he walked over to the cowering wolf and sniffed her face.

Blackie, the female wolf, whined in gentle tones. Somehow this made Ruff feel good. He also liked the smell of the other wolf. He licked her face in friendship.

Then Blackie stood up and bounded away. She looked back at Ruff, whining for him to follow her. Ruff gave a happy bark and raced after her. They touched noses. Soon they reached the top of a rise and ran down the other side.

There Ruff and Blackie came upon some other wolves. The black wolf belonged to their pack. They were her family. The large gray with a creamy ruff was her father. The smaller wolf next to him was his mate, Blackie's mother. The others were the black wolf's brothers and sisters. The wolf family had wandered down from the north, hunting for food.

Ruff stood very still as the large gray leader came toward him. The gray slowly sniffed at Ruff. Then Ruff sniffed the leader, all the time wagging his tail in friendliness. Finally the leader walked away, and the other wolves came up to Ruff. Ruff made no move that was unfriendly. At last the wolves seemed to be no longer interested in this stranger and walked away.

Forgetting all about Blackie, Ruff turned around, too. He went back to the ranch. But the next night he met the black female again. This time the other wolves were nowhere near. So together Blackie and Ruff romped and played in the snow.

Suddenly Blackie put her head down on her front paws and sprang up at Ruff. Ruff tried to avoid her charge and tumbled in a snowbank. Blackie nipped his flank playfully and dashed away. Ruff bounded after her. Although she was much smaller than Ruff, she was just as fast. It was not easy for Ruff to catch up to her. When he finally caught up, he nipped her flank. This game was repeated over and over. Sometimes Blackie would hide behind a snowbank and spring out at Ruff. Although Ruff would act surprised, he always knew where she was. Then the wolves would shake the snow from their fur and run off together.

One evening after supper, Mrs. Logue looked up from her sewing. She silently watched Jim. Her son was sitting near the fireplace, his brow wrinkled in thought.

Feeling his mother's eyes on him, Jim suddenly looked up and grinned. But before he could speak, a long wailing howl broke through the dusk.

Both Mrs. Logue and Jim were familiar with Ruff's strange wolf song. It usually signaled the beginning of his nightly patrol. Unconsciously, both had been waiting for it. They had come to like the wild, dismal, haunting howl that brought such fear into the hearts of the other ranchers. But tonight Ruff's howl was answered by another coming from the hills just north of the ranch. It was Blackie calling to her mate. Every evening Blackie had come closer and closer to the Logue ranch to meet her mate.

Jim glanced uneasily at his mother as Blackie's call died away.

Mrs. Logue looked out of the window and then back down at her sewing. "I'm sure that Ruff has a mate," she said. "Don't you think"—the woman searched for the right words—"don't you think Ruff has changed?" she asked her son.

Jim didn't want to admit it, but he knew it was true. Although Ruff was still as affectionate and loyal as ever, he had changed. Jim knew that Ruff was gone most of the night now. The wolf napped almost all day. He no longer romped and played with Queenie. Neither did he seem as anxious to go on his afternoon walks with Jim and Queenie.

Mrs. Logue's gentle voice broke into Jim's thoughts. "If you want to keep Ruff, you'll have to pen him up at night."

Jim stared at the fire, watching the flickering flames dance and sputter. Thinking of how much the wolf hated to be kept in the wire pen, Jim thought to himself, "Not yet, Ruff. Not just yet."

Ruff, unaware that Jim and his mother were discussing his future, had raced off to meet Blackie. Although the wolf did not know it, Blackie would have whelps in about two months. But instinct did tell him that he and Blackie must find a den.

That night they found a snug hollow in the snow under a fir. The hole was an abandoned coyote den. Ruff and Blackie worked together making the den larger. When they were through, the entrance to the den was about a foot and a half in diameter. An eight-foot tunnel led to an inner chamber. This chamber was made large enough so that the wolves could stand up.

Then Blackie taught Ruff how to kill deer. Although Ruff had learned a lot from Queenie about how to hunt, Ruff had never felt the need to kill for food. But now somehow Ruff knew that Blackie and he would need plenty of food in the coming months.

After a few tries, Ruff and Blackie worked well as a team. Together they would stalk the deer, trying to pick one that seemed less agile than the others. Finding a likely prospect, Blackie would snarl and growl at the deer's face. Ruff would attack it from the rear. When the deer was exhausted, Ruff would grab its throat and kill it. After they had eaten all they wanted, Ruff would bury the rest in the snow.

Every night he and Blackie hunted for food. Toward morning they came back to the den and settled down to rest. But after a while Ruff would get restless. His love for Jim was too strong, and he would leave Blackie and go home to the ranch.

One evening Ruff came back to the ranch earlier than usual. In the house, a lamp was still burning. Ruff went to the kitchen door and whined.

"Well, you're back early," Jim said as he opened the door. "Come on, I'll put you to bed."

Jim put on his jacket and walked to the barn with Ruff. When the boy opened the door, Queenie woke up. Jim gave the collie and the wolf a hug and closed the door. Queenie curled up on a pile of hay and went back to sleep. Ruff dropped down at her side. After a while he went to sleep, too.

The lone wolf watching from the ridge had seen Ruff's passage through the valley. He had seen the light go off in the house. The old white wolf was Ruff's father. Ever since his mate had been killed by Mr. Diggs, the old male had not joined up with any other wolf pack. He had hunted alone.

Hunting alone was hard work. The bullet had left his right front leg useless. Besides, he was very old and was not as strong as he had once been. No longer was he able to catch the fleet deer and elk or even rabbits and mice. He had had nothing to eat for the past week.

The old wolf rose from the ground and sniffed the air. The scent of man was strong. Although the wolf feared man, the need for food was stronger.

Limping on his three good legs, the wolf made his way cautiously down the trail toward the sheep pens. Every once in a while he stopped to sniff the air. When he came to the sheep, he quietly crawled under the bottom rail of the pen and lay motionless in the snow. Finally one of the sheep walked by him, and the large white wolf sprang at its throat. Although the old male had few good teeth left, his jaws were still powerful. The old wolf hung on until he had choked the life out of the sheep.

The white wolf dragged the sheep out of the pen. Then, casting quick looks around him, he started tearing at the fresh meat.

6
RUFF
MAKES A CHOICE

THE NEXT MORNING was clear but bitterly cold. Jim's teeth chattered as he climbed out of bed and quickly dressed in his warmest clothes. Then he went downstairs and out the back door. Queenie and Ruff, ·who had been listening for the back door to slam shut, raced out of the barn to meet him.

The dog and wolf followed him when Jim went out to pitch hay to the sheep. But suddenly Ruff stopped and sniffed the air. Then he gave a sharp bark and started sniffing the ground. Queenie had smelled something too, for she darted after Ruff.

Whistling softly, the boy followed the two animals along the fence of the sheep pen. Suddenly the whistle died on Jim's lips. Before him were the large wolf tracks and the bright red stains in the snow. A dozen yards farther on, Jim found the remains of the wolf's feast. There wasn't much left of the sheep—just some bones and the wooly pelt. Anger swept through the boy as he saw that one of the Hampshires had been killed. By now Jim's trust in Ruff was so great that not once did he think that Ruff might have been the killer.

After breakfast Jim got his rifle and skis. Mrs. Logue wiped her hands on her apron and watched Jim put on a heavy jacket.

"There's a stockmen's meeting tonight at the Diggs' ranch," she reminded him. "Larry Harwood thinks you should go—in case someone talks about Ruff."

Jim nodded and started out the door. But then he turned back. "If I'm not back in time . . ."

"I'll go," Mrs. Logue said and smiled.

Jim had no trouble following the tracks of the wolf in the snow. The wolf had made no attempt to conceal his trail. Following the style of the Finnish people who had first settled the valley, Jim used his skis as if they were skates. In this way he could go very fast.

Queenie and Ruff were following the wolf's scent. Soon Ruff started to bay in deep, rapid barks. Queenie bayed, too. They were hot on the scent of the wolf.

On the crest of a distant rise, the white male wolf was resting. Suddenly he lifted his head. He heard a wolf's cry and a dog's bark. The old wolf slowly got to his feet. Although he was not afraid, neither did he want to fight. He turned and started down the ridge. Although he had only three good legs, the wolf could run fairly fast.

The old male ran into the ravine. He looked up at the den he had shared with his mate for over twelve years. The white wolf had often come back, still searching for his mate. Behind him, he heard the barks growing louder and louder.

The old wolf circled the ravine and came out on the edge of the cliff. His breath came in long rasping gasps, shaking the wolf's whole body. He was very tired— more tired than he had ever felt before. The white wolf lifted his head and looked up at the sky, his yellow eyes clouded. Then he gave a strange howl.

As Jim followed the barking animals, he soon realized that they were heading toward the wolf den that had been Ruff's first home. He hoped the old white male wasn't the killer. He didn't want to kill Ruff's father.

Ruff and Queenie dashed into the ravine and up the slope to the den. But when Jim reached the ravine, he realized that something was wrong. Although Ruff and Queenie were barking at something on the narrow ledge, there was no answering sound.

As Ruff and Queenie made no move to leave the ledge, Jim decided to climb up the slope. When he reached the ledge, he found Ruff's father. The old white wolf was dead!

Jim pulled Queenie and Ruff off the ledge and started down the slope, leaving the old wolf to guard the den in death as he had done in life.

Jim started out of the ravine, but he didn't head toward home. He wanted to be alone. He wanted to think. He headed north—toward the high, jagged mountains.

As Jim skied along, he thought about the old white wolf. "What had brought the old fellow back to the den?" the boy thought to himself. "Was it just habit? Or was the wolf so devoted to his mate that he had returned to the den searching for her?" Somehow it bothered the boy to find the white wolf at the den.

The sun was beginning to set as Jim reached the top of a high ridge. For a moment he looked down the steep slope. It was over half a mile long. Then he gave himself a push and went flying down the hill.

The boy gasped for breath as the sudden rush of wind hit his face. His face burned, but he didn't slacken his great speed. Finally the boy stopped thinking about the dead wolf. He concentrated on his thrilling ride. As he skied faster and faster, his spirits began to lift. Behind him he could hear the excited barks of Queenie and Ruff as they plunged down the slope after him. Suddenly Jim began to check his speed. He didn't want this ride to end too quickly.

All at once Jim found himself spinning abruptly around. A terrible pain went through his left leg and he fell heavily to the ground. Then everything went black.

CAPOZIO

Ruff and Queenie had seen Jim fall. Barking frantically, they half ran and half slid down the slope to the boy's side. Both of them knew that something was wrong.

Finally Jim groaned and opened his eyes. Queenie and Ruff were standing over him, licking his face and whining. For a moment the boy didn't know what had happened and started to sit up. Gasping at the sharp pain in his leg, Jim fell back on the snow. He realized that he had broken his leg.

All at once Jim began to feel afraid. Trying not to move his leg, he felt around in the snow for his rifle. He raised himself up on his elbow and looked around. Thinking that the gun might have rolled down the hill, Jim started to inch his way down the slope looking for it. Finally, his strength exhausted, the boy had to give up. He lay back on the snow and closed his eyes.

Queenie and Ruff had sat silently watching Jim's struggle. Now they came back to his side. Queenie shoved her nose against Jim's arm, and Ruff laid his paw on Jim's chest.

Jim opened his eyes and gave each animal a long hug. "If I am to be saved," he said thoughtfully, "you will have to help me."

Then, leaning on his elbow, he looked at Queenie and pointed toward home. "Queenie, go home! Fetch Mom!"

The collie cocked her head.

"Queenie, fetch Mom! Go fetch Mom!" Jim commanded in a stern voice.

Queenie backed off slowly. Then she whined.

"Go home, girl," Jim said, his voice pleading. "Ruff will stay here. Go home, Queenie!"

Then the black-and-white collie turned and started slowly down the mountain. Halfway to the bottom, she looked back up at Jim. Then she turned and continued down the slope.

Ruff rested his head on his paws and stretched out next to Jim. As night closed in on them, the nearness of the wolf's body helped to keep Jim warm.

A full moon had risen. Jim watched the twinkling stars. He tried to keep from thinking what would happen if Queenie did not go home. Instead, he tried to imagine where the dog might be. He thought of the familiar landmarks she would pass on her journey to the ranch. Maybe she was already running through the meadow where he had found the orphaned fawn. Perhaps she was trotting across the old bridge over a mountain stream. Possibly she was already barking at the ranch door.

All at once Ruff jerked up his head. The wolf cocked his head and listened intently. Then he sat up and stared at the woods. Jim followed the wolf's gaze to the forest, but the boy could neither see nor hear anything.

Suddenly the wolf rose to his feet. His yellow eyes were still fixed intently on the dark woods. Then Jim saw a big gray wolf walk into the open. Behind him were four more wolves.

The big leader lifted his head and sniffed the cold air. He smelled man. He looked over at the two figures in the snow and sniffed again. Then the leader took a few steps forward. The wolves behind him also moved forward, walking in the big gray's tracks.

Ruff, still standing at Jim's side, had watched curiously. But when the leader took another step forward, Ruff suddenly growled savagely.

Jim no longer felt the pain in his leg. He was gazing spellbound at Ruff.

Ruff's lips were curled into a vicious snarl. His yellow eyes glowed with hate. Between powerful jaws, his long razor-sharp fangs gleamed in the moonlight. His ears were pressed flat against his head. His great ruff stood up around his neck, framing the wolf's ferocious head. In a second Ruff had changed into a savage beast.

The wolf leader paused, then took another step forward. When the leader and Ruff were only a few feet apart, Ruff crouched in the snow. His huge body was tense, his eyes watchful.

Suddenly the leader sprang forward. Ruff met him head on. Ruff's greater weight and size knocked the other wolf on his side. Growling, Ruff tried for the leader's throat, but the leader jumped aside quickly. Ruff's powerful jaws closed instead on the wolf's right shoulder. Putting all his power into the effort, Ruff threw his weight to the left and let go. The leader went sprawling down the steep slope. He slid a good forty feet down the surface of the frozen snow before he gained his footing.

Then another wolf moved in to attack Ruff. But in an instant Ruff had also sent him spinning down the slope.

The remaining wolves did not move. Ruff stood waiting as the leader and the other wolf climbed back up the slope.

Suddenly another wolf trotted out of the woods and started across the side of the mountain. It was Blackie. Ever since sunset she had been searching for her mate. She whined softly as she moved toward Ruff. When she was next to him, she jumped up and put her paws on Ruff's shoulders and licked his face. Ruff paid no attention to her. His ears flat against his head, he tensely watched the other wolves.

As the leader moved forward again, Blackie suddenly whirled and bared her teeth. The leader, her father, seemed surprised and dropped back. If the battle were to begin again, Blackie would fight on Ruff's side.

Finally the leader whined and started wagging his tail. Ruff stiffened as the leader walked slowly forward, but Ruff made no attempt to attack. Then the leader sniffed Ruff's face and put his paw on Ruff's shoulder in friendship. The other wolves also moved forward, wagging their tails.

Jim had been so fascinated by what was happening that the boy had forgotten his fear. Now as he saw that Ruff had become friends with the other wolves, he began to worry. Had Ruff gone over to the wolves? Would they tear him to pieces?

At that moment one of the male wolves began to sniff his way toward Jim. Quickly Ruff sprang between Jim and the young male. He wrinkled his upper lip and let out a deep, fierce growl. The young male backed off. Then he sat down and howled. The other wolves joined in. Finally Ruff and Blackie added their song. The wolves' howling chorus could be heard for miles.

Suddenly a loud shout rang out from below, and the wolves suddenly fell silent. Then the wolf pack whirled and dashed into the forest. Although Blackie was frightened, too, she stopped at the edge of the timber. There she sat down and anxiously watched her mate.

Jim looked down the slope. He saw two men walking up the mountain. Ruff ran to meet Queenie, who was bounding up the slope. Together the dog and wolf romped around in joy. Then they ran over to Jim.

A few minutes later Frank Diggs and Larry Harwood were at Jim's side.

"Am I glad to see you!" Jim exclaimed. "I don't know how you got here, but I'm sure glad you did!"

"You have a mighty smart dog there," Mr. Diggs said. "Your mother was at the stockmen's meeting when Queenie came barking at the door. Evidently, Queenie followed your mother's scent all the way to my ranch."

"Sadie wanted to come, too," Larry Harwood said, "but we wouldn't let her. We'll have you home before you know it."

"Ruff and Queenie both saved my life," Jim told the two men. He put an arm around each of the animals. "Queenie went for help, and Ruff saved me from a pack of wolves. You should have seen him fight to protect me!"

Frank Diggs gave the wolf a quick glance of admiration.

"Let's get you down to the sled," Larry Harwood said. He and Mr. Diggs moved over to Jim. At that moment Ruff bounded up the slope.

"Ruff!" Jim called. "Come here!"

Ruff stopped and looked back at Jim.

"Come, Ruff," Jim called.

Ruff sat down and howled. He looked at Blackie. Then he looked at Jim.

Jim could see that the wolf did not know what to do. The animal was torn between two loyalties—between two homes.

Jim raised himself up on his elbow and called in a stern voice, "Ruff! Come here!"

At the harsh command, Ruff rose and obediently walked to the boy.

Jim threw his arms around the gray wolf's neck and held the wolf tightly. The temptation was strong to grab Ruff's collar and take him back to the ranch. "Even if Ruff has to be penned," he told himself, "it would be better than having no wolf at all!"

Then Jim knew he couldn't do it. The wolf was born to run free. The boy reached up and took off Ruff's leather collar.

"Go on, Ruff," Jim said sadly. "Take your black mate and go far away from here. Take her into the mountains far away from this valley. Don't ever come back, Ruff. You're free now. Go on home."

For a few minutes Ruff hesitated. He looked at Jim and whined. Then he turned and looked at Blackie, who was waiting nervously near the woods. Ruff gave Jim one long last look. Then he turned and ran toward the black wolf.

As Jim and the two men watched, Ruff and Blackie touched noses and then, shoulder to shoulder, glided into the dark forest.

EXERCISES

Chapter One

THE WOLF DEN

Choose the right ending for each of these sentences.

1. The Logue ranch was at the northern tip of a long valley that was called
   a)   Cascade Valley.
   b)   Long Valley.
   c)   River Valley.

2. After the spring lambs were born, Jim would
   a)   move the sheep to the mountains.
   b)   put the lambs in a pen.
   c)   move the sheep to the river.

3. The Hampshire rams were bought
   a)   because they didn't cost very much money.
   b)   in order to improve the sheep flock.
   c)   so they could be fattened for market.

4. When Queenie pressed her nose against Jim's hand, her nose
   a)   felt warm.
   b)   felt cold.
   c)   was neither warm nor cold.

5. The color of Jim's dog was
   a)   brown and black.
   b)   brown.
   c)   black and white.

6. The job that Mr. Harwood gave Jim was to
   a) find a wolf den.
   b) set out coyote traps.
   c) shoot wolves.

7. The hunting trail of a wolf is called a
   a) deer path.
   b) wolf runway.
   c) cattle trail.

8. In his hunt for the wolf den Jim decided to
   a) look everywhere.
   b) look along the riverbank.
   c) pick out a few likely spots and watch them closely.

9. Mr. Diggs said that the wolves and other predators
   a) don't like to eat wild game.
   b) would kill livestock for food.
   c) like to kill cattle and sheep for the fun of it.

10. After Mr. Diggs had gone away, Queenie found
    a) a rockchuck.
    b) the gray female still alive.
    c) a wolf pup that had not been killed.

Chapter Two
A NEW HOME

Choose the right ending for each of these sentences.

1. When Mrs. Logue saw the little wolf pup,
   a) she said it was a vicious wolf.
   b) she said it did not look very vicious.
   c) the whelp barked at her.

2. When Mrs. Logue saw that the wolf pup's eyes were not open, she said
   a) the pup was three weeks old.
   b) the pup would not live.
   c) Jim would have to feed the pup in the middle of the night.

3. Jim named the little wolf pup Ruff because
   a) full-grown male wolves have a ruff.
   b) the little pup was very rough when he played.
   c) the pup chewed the nipple of his milk bottle.

4. Ruff's stomach stopped hurting when
   a) Queenie licked Ruff's stomach and pressed it with her nose.
   b) Jim burped Ruff like a baby.
   c) Mrs. Logue gave the pup more milk.

5. By September Ruff's eyes were
   a) light blue.
   b) deep brown.
   c) yellow.

6. Although Ruff was almost three feet long from his nose to the tip of his tail, Jim would not let him run free because
   a) the coyotes might kill him.
   b) he might run away.
   c) he would howl forlornly.

7. Jim was surprised that Ruff
   a) shook the rockchuck so hard.
   b) ate the tough old rockchuck.
   c) let the rockchuck go.

8. Mrs. Logue said that, if Ruff kept eating as he had been,
   a) he would become very thin.
   b) she would have to spend the whole day cooking for him.
   c) he would have to be fed with the horses.

9. To Ruff, hunting and catching rockchucks was
   a) how he got his food.
   b) hard work.
   c) a game.

10. When Ruff ran up the trail after Mrs. Logue had let him out of his pen, Queenie
    a) ran after him.
    b) sat down and howled.
    c) stayed in the yard.

Chapter Three
TRAPPED!

Choose the right ending for each of these sentences.

1. Queenie and Ruff chased a cottontail
   a) up the riverbank and across the fields.
   b) into a small willow thicket.
   c) into the tall grass by the river.

2. When Ruff found a narrow entrance to the thicket, he
   a) sniffed the ground around the opening.
   b) knew there must be traps in the narrow entrance.
   c) sat down and howled.

3. When Queenie ran to the narrow opening in the willow thicket, she
   a) saw Ruff eating the cottontail.
   b) could not see Ruff anywhere.
   c) saw at once that Ruff was caught in a trap.

4. Queenie attacked the coyote, and then she
   a) killed it.
   b) let it go.
   c) and the coyote rolled into the river.

5. When Mr. Diggs first saw Queenie, he thought
   a) a sheep might be caught in the thicket.
   b) Ruff might be caught in a trap.
   c) Jim Logue might be in some kind of trouble.

6. Mr. Diggs did not shoot Ruff because
   a) the rancher felt sorry for him.
   b) the rancher was afraid the bullet might hit Queenie.
   c) Queenie's manner made him change his mind.

7. At first Mr. Diggs could not understand why Queenie was friendly with a wolf. Then the thought came to him that
   a) Queenie was part wolf herself.
   b) Jim had found one of the gray wolf's pups.
   c) Queenie would help any trapped animal.

8. Jim was surprised to see Ruff sitting
   a) on the rancher's horse.
   b) in Mr. Diggs' wagon.
   c) in the pen next to the barn.

9. When Ruff grabbed Jim's arm between his powerful jaws, Jim told Mr. Diggs
   a) that it was the wolf's way of showing affection.
   b) to shoot Ruff quick before he bit off Jim's arm.
   c) to pull Ruff's jaws apart.

10. When the rancher warned Jim that Ruff might kill the Logues' fine sheep, Jim said,
    a) "I think you may be right, Mr. Diggs."
    b) "Ruff has never even growled at a sheep, sir. He *wouldn't* kill a sheep!"
    c) "Mr. Harwood told me the same thing."

Chapter Four

MORE TROUBLE

Choose the right ending for each of these sentences.

1. When Ruff was a year old, he
    a) was twenty-seven inches high at the shoulder.
    b) weighed eighty-five pounds.
    c) was still smaller than Queenie.

2. Mr. Harwood told Mrs. Logue and Jim that the stockmen's association was raising money to
    a) build a powerhouse at Cascade River Falls.
    b) pay a bounty on each wolf or coyote killed.
    c) loan to ranchers to buy Hampshire sheep.

3. When Mr. Harwood told the ranchers that wolves help to keep wild game strong, the ranchers
    a) wouldn't listen.
    b) decided not to kill wolves.
    c) said that the main problem was coyotes.

4. The Logues had not lost any stock because
    a) predators did not like sheep.
    b) the Logues were too far from the river.
    c) Ruff was a good watchdog.

5. Queenie tried to stop Ruff from eating the poisoned sheep, but
    a) Ruff drove her off.
    b) some coyotes scared her away.
    c) Jim called her back before she could stop Ruff.

6. When Jim found he could not carry Ruff, he
   a) sent Queenie home to fetch Mrs. Logue.
   b) gave up and waited for Ruff to die.
   c) left Queenie to guard Ruff and ran home to get the wagon.

7. When the buckboard broke down, Mrs. Logue said,
   a) "We will just have to give up, I guess."
   b) "We should be able to bring Ruff home on a horse."
   c) "We will have to fix the buckboard as soon as we can."

8. When Jim asked his mother where she was going with Ruff, she said she was going
   a) home as fast as she could.
   b) to the river.
   c) to Larry Harwood for help.

9. When Jim carried Ruff into the water, the wolf
   a) struggled to get away.
   b) trembled all over.
   c) began to drink.

10. After Jim and Mrs. Logue took Ruff home,
    a) Ruff was as good as ever in a few hours.
    b) Mrs. Logue had to nurse him for several days.
    c) Ruff died, and they buried him in the backyard.

Chapter Five
THE BLACK WOLF

Choose the right ending for each of these sentences.

1. The boy's love for the wolf deepened,
    a) but the wolf showed no fondness for the boy.
    b) and the wolf showed genuine fondness for the boy.
    c) but Queenie did not like the boy to show fondness for the wolf.

2. The ranchers of the valley were worried because
    a) never had there been so few deer and elk in the valley.
    b) they were afraid of the howls of the wolves.
    c) the howls of the wolves disturbed their sleep.

3. At three years old, Ruff weighed
    a) three hundred pounds.
    b) one hundred fifty pounds.
    c) one hundred pounds.

4. One bright moonlight night Ruff
    a) met a mountain lion.
    b) met a female wolf.
    c) heard Jim call him.

5. The wolves that Blackie and Ruff met
    a) were Blackie's family.
    b) fought Ruff.
    c) were disliked by Ruff.

6. Ruff signaled the beginning of his nightly patrol of the Logue ranch by
   a) barking loudly.
   b) a long wailing howl.
   c) scratching on the kitchen door.

7. Mrs. Logue said to Jim that if he wanted to keep Ruff he would have to
   a) get rid of Queenie.
   b) find a den for him.
   c) pen Ruff up at night.

8. Ruff had never felt the need to kill for food, so Blackie
   a) taught him to kill deer.
   b) learned to eat cooked food herself.
   c) ran off with another wolf.

9. The old white wolf was Ruff's
   a) brother.
   b) mother.
   c) father.

10. When the old white wolf came to the sheep pen, he
    a) crawled under the bottom rail and lay motionless in the snow.
    b) crawled under the bottom rail and sprang among the sheep.
    c) stood outside because he had seen the light go off in the house.

Chapter Six
RUFF MAKES A CHOICE

Choose the right ending for each of these sentences.

1. When Jim followed Ruff and Queenie along the fence of the sheep pen, he
   a) whistled to Ruff and Queenie.
   b) found one of the Hampshires had been killed.
   c) was angry because Queenie was sniffing the ground.

2. Jim's mother said that Larry Harwood thought Jim should go to the stockmen's meeting
   a) in case someone talked about Ruff.
   b) in case the question of raising Hampshire sheep came up.
   c) to find out about the new bounty on coyotes.

3. The old white male wolf
   a) concealed his trail so well that Jim could not find it.
   b) ran off to meet some other wolves.
   c) made no attempt to conceal his trail.

4. When the old white wolf heard Queenie's bark and Ruff's cry, he
   a) hid in some huckleberry bushes.
   b) went back to the ravine where he and his mate had had their den.
   c) decided to stay and fight the dog and wolf.

5. When Jim reached the ravine, he found Ruff and Queenie barking at something on the narrow ledge. It was the
   a) old white wolf, who was facing them with his teeth bared.
   b) old white wolf, who was dead.
   c) black female.

6. When Jim fell down while he was skiing, he
   a) did not know what had happened to him at first.
   b) thought a hunter had accidentally shot him.
   c) thought he had broken a ski.

7. When Jim realized his leg was broken, he
   a) sent Ruff home for help.
   b) sent Queenie home for help.
   c) was afraid Ruff would tear him to pieces.

8. Suddenly Ruff rose to his feet, his yellow eyes fixed intently on the dark woods. Then Jim saw a
   a) deer walk from the woods into the moonlight.
   b) band of coyotes on the ledge above him.
   c) big gray wolf walk into the open.

9. When Jim saw that the wolves and Ruff had become friends, he was afraid
   a) Ruff would let the wolves tear him to pieces.
   b) the wolves really were not friendly and would wait for a chance to kill Ruff.
   c) Ruff had been badly hurt.

10. When Frank Diggs and Larry Harwood started to take Jim home,
    a) Jim called Ruff to him and, holding his leather collar, made Ruff come back to the ranch.
    b) Jim took off Ruff's leather collar and told him to take his black mate far away into the mountains.
    c) Ruff ran on ahead with Queenie toward the ranch house.

THE DOG FAMILY

THE WOLF is a member of the dog family. Like the dog, the wolf wags its tail when it is happy, snarls when it is angry, barks when it is excited, and howls when it is lonely. But while the dog is called "man's best friend," the wolf has always been considered to be man's mortal enemy. However, the chief difference between the wolf and the dog is that the wolf is wild while the dog is tame.

WOLF

COYOTE

There are other wild dogs besides the wolf. The coyote belongs to the dog family, too. Sometimes a wolf is mistaken for a coyote. The wolf, however, is a larger animal with a heavier, rounder muzzle and short, rounded ears. The coyote, on the other hand, has many fox-like features, such as a long slim muzzle and large pointed ears.

The fox is another wild dog, although a more distant relative. While the wolf and coyote will mate with a dog, the fox will not.

The wolf, dog, coyote, and fox are also related to other animals through ancient ancestors that lived about fifty million years ago. These ancestors, known as the Miacidae, were small tree-climbing mammals. They were meat-eaters. Animals that eat meat are called carnivores. Wolves, dogs, coyotes, and foxes are carnivores. So are raccoons, bears, and cats.

FOX

DOG

Wolves eat any kind of meat they can find—caribou, moose, ground squirrels, rabbits, mice, deer, and elk. They also feed on fish and domestic livestock. They, as well as coyotes and bears, also eat carrion—the rotting flesh of dead animals. A wolf will also bury food for a later meal. These caches are visited by coyotes, foxes, and bears.

Wolves and many other carnivores also eat plants. Wolves and coyotes will eat wild grapes and plums. In British Columbia, during certain times of the year, some wolves were found to live mainly on berries. The gray wolf has even been known to eat watermelons. Furthermore, it seems to have the ability to pick out the melons that are ripe!

RED WOLF

There are two main types of wolves found in North America—the red and the gray. The red wolf is considered to be uniquely American. The gray, on the other hand, has close relatives in other parts of the world. The red wolf is much smaller than the gray, weighing as little as 30 pounds; the gray wolf may weigh as much as 175 pounds. At one time the red wolf ranged over most of the southern United States. Now, however, only a few red wolves are still found in Texas and the Mississippi Valley.

Although called "gray," the gray wolf, or timber wolf, comes in a variety of colors from pure white to jet black, as well as many shades in between. Gray, however, seems to be the most common color. White

GRAY WOLF

wolves are found more often in the Arctic, but black wolves are found there, too.

The gray wolf is from 26 to 38 inches in height and weighs between 60 and 175 pounds. Some gray wolves have reached a length of eight feet from nose to tail. These larger wolves are usually found in Alaska and Canada.

The wolf is a devoted parent, a good provider, and a faithful, affectionate mate. It first mates at two or three years of age and usually has the same mate for life. Mating takes place between January and March. In about two months the whelps are born. The wolves

WOLVES ARE DEVOTED PARENTS

use a den while raising their young. The litter averages seven pups. On the ninth day, the pups' eyes open. The male brings the female food because she will not leave the den while the whelps are young.

At weaning time, when the pups are around eight weeks old, the parents bring food for the pups to eat. On the hunt, the parents eat heavily of their kill. When they return to the den, they disgorge part of what they have eaten for the pups. They also bring back small animals and bones for the young to chew on. When the pups are old enough, they are taught by their parents how to hunt.

Besides the parents and the young, other wolves may live at the den. Usually these are older animals. They will take care of the young while the parents are hunting. Whelps over a year old are sometimes still found with the family group. Two or more families, all of whom are related, may form a large family group. During the off-mating period, wolf families may join into wolf packs to hunt for food.

Wolves prefer to do their hunting at night. On a hunt, wolves usually test each herd of game they find. If they notice an ill or weak animal, they will kill it. In this manner the wolves help to keep the wild game in good condition. Only healthy animals are left to breed and keep the herds strong.

Wolves follow a regular established route on their hunt for food. This hunting trail is called a wolf runway. Since wolves prefer to travel in open country, part of their runway may be a cattle trail or an old road. Part of it may go through a canyon or cross the top of a ridge. One runway was found to follow a seldom-traveled highway. At places along the runway are high points from which the wolves can look around.

In some places the runway may be a few feet wide. At other places the runway may be a mile or more in width. Some runways have been known to be ten miles wide.

The shape of the runway is somewhat like a circle

and may be twenty to sixty miles across. Some runways have been known to be as long as two hundred miles. Generally, wolves travel their runways in a counter-clockwise direction. Why this is true is not known.

A wolf marks out its runway with a series of scent posts. A scent post may be a tree, stump, clump of brush, or a shrub. On these places the wolf deposits its scent. Another wolf can read a scent post as well as a man can read a book. It can tell many things about the wolf that had been there—whether it was sick or well, hungry or well-fed, male or female, even whether it was angry or happy!

Wolves have a language they use to communicate with one another. Some human beings have claimed that they understand this "language" and are able to talk to the wolves. Not only that, they claim that the wolves talk back!

Wolves have a great many sounds in their vocabulary. The female whines softly to her whelps. During the mating season, a lonesome wailing howl is heard. A loud, deep, throaty howl is used to call the pack together for the chase. As the wolves trail their prey, their barks become deep and rapid, similar to the sounds made by a pack of hounds on a hot scent. Then as their teeth sink into a victim's throat, they snarl deeply, much as an angry bulldog does.

People never forget the lonesome wailing howls that are heard when a group of wolves gather together on a cold winter night. Each wolf barks and howls differently from the others. Each time it howls, the tone and pitch change. One wolf is able to utter so many different sounds that one wolf can sound like several, and a few wolves can seem like fifty!

As more settlers moved deeper and deeper into the wilderness, it was fated that they should come into conflict with the wolf. Unlike other animals that were able to retreat in the face of man's steady advance, wolves were unable to adjust to this new menace. They stayed where they were. In the place of wild game, the wolves killed cattle, sheep, and horses. So much livestock was destroyed by wolves that the ranchers got together and formed stockmen's associations. The associations paid bounties for wolves. Finally the counties and states started paying bounties, too. Even the United States appointed official wolf hunters.

In its long fight with man, the wolf has been the loser. Once thousands of wolves ranged throughout the United States. Today, except for Alaska and some remote areas of the states, the wolf is extremely uncommon.

What kind of an animal is the wolf? Is it the fierce, ruthless, wanton killer that most people believe? Perhaps Ernest Thompson Seton's description of the wolf is closer to the truth. Mr. Seton was a great naturalist who wrote many stories about wolves. In his book *Mainly About Wolves,* he says:

Our traditional picture of the wolf presents an odious creature, a monster of cruelty and destruction; actuated by nothing higher than a gluttonous appetite for food.

Yet I have seen wolves that were dainty as deer in matters of diet. I have learned of wolves whose master trait was wisdom.

I have known of wolves whose animating force was the spirit of adventure. I have been told of wolves whose strongest motivation was revenge.

I have met many a wolf whose overwhelming motive was the love of its little ones. I have seen wolves whose master passion was devotion to a dearly loved mate. I have heard of wolves who made a brotherhood pact, an affectionate alliance with some wholly different animal.

And I have knowledge of one wolf at least whose chiefest binding urge in life was loving devotion to his blind and helpless old mother.[1]

Perhaps the wolf is not such a bad fellow after all. Maybe it has been misunderstood.

[1] Ernest Thompson Seton, *Mainly About Wolves* (New York, Charles Scribner's Sons, 1937).